By

Meghan, The Duchess of Sussex

Pictures by Christian Robinson

PUFFIN BOOKS

UK | USA | Canada | Ireland | Australia | India | New Zealand | South Africa

Puffin Books is part of the Penguin Random House group of companies whose addresses can be found at global.penguinrandomhouse.com.

www.penguin.co.uk www.puffin.co.uk www.ladybird.co.uk

Penguin Random House UK

First published in the United States by Random House Children's Books, a division of Penguin Random house LLC, New York 2021
Published in Great Britain by Puffin Books 2021

A CIP catalogue record for this book is available from the British Library

All correspondence to Puffin Books, Penguin Random House Children's, One Embassy Gardens, 8 Viaduct Gardens, London SW11 7BW

The authorized representative in the EEA is Penguin Random House Ireland, Morrison Chambers, 32 Nassau Street, Dublin DO2 YH68

ISBN: 978-0-241-54221-7

The artist used acrylic paint, coloured pencil, and a bit of digital manipulation to create the illustrations for this book.
The text of this book is set in 17-point Jazmin. Interior design by Martha Rago and Christian Robinson.

Printed and bound in Italy / 001

For the man and the boy
who make my heart go
pump-pump

This is your bench
Where life will begin
For you and our son
Our baby, our kin.

This is your bench
Where you'll witness great joy.

From here you will rest
See the growth of our boy.

He'll learn to ride a bike
As you watch on with pride.

He’ll run and he’ll fall
And he’ll take it in stride.

You'll love him.
You'll listen.
You'll be his supporter.

When life feels in shambles

You'll help him find order.

You'll sit on this bench
As his giving tree.

Some days he may cry
Perched there on your knee.

He'll feel happiness, sorrow
One day be heartbroken.

You'll tell him "I love you"
Those words always spoken.

This is your bench
For papa and son . . .

To celebrate joys
And victories won.

And here in the window
I'll have tears of great joy . . .

Looking out at My Love
And our beautiful boy.

Right there on your bench
The place you'll call home . . .

With daddy and son . . .

Where you'll never be 'lone.

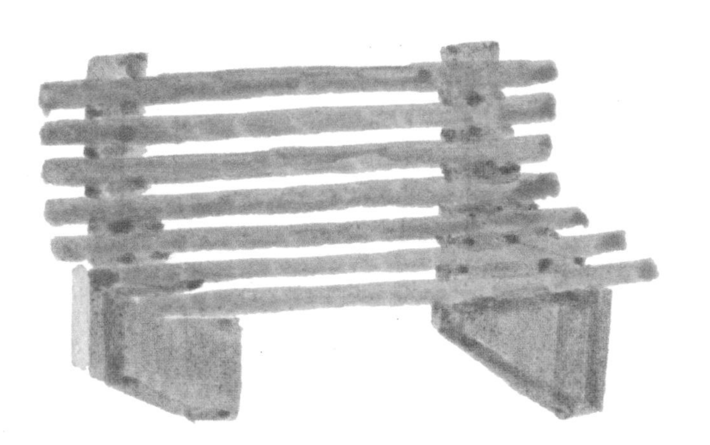

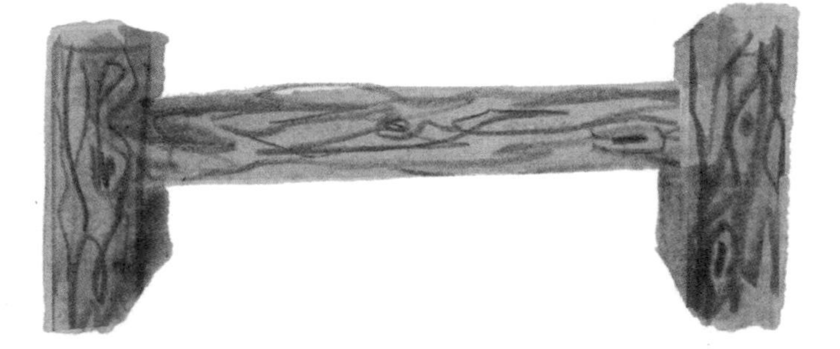